For Charlotte

First published by Candlewick Press

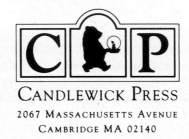

CANDLEWICK PRESS
2067 MASSACHUSETTS AVENUE
CAMBRIDGE MA 02140

ISBN 0-590-99284-8

Copyright © 1994 by Virginia Austin.
All rights reserved. Published by Scholastic Inc., 555 Broadway, New York, NY 10012,
by arrangement with Candlewick Press.

20 19 18 17 16 15   8 9/0

Printed in the U.S.A.

First Scholastic printing, September 1996

The pictures in this book were done in pencil and watercolor.

Say Please

Virginia Austin

CANDLEWICK PRESS
CAMBRIDGE, MASSACHUSETTS

The dog said,
"Throw my ball,
woof woof
please."

"Woof woof thank you."

The ducks said,
"Give us some bread,
quack quack
please."

"Quack quack
thank you."

The cat said,
"Give me some milk,
meow meow
please."

"She said please."

"Purr purr
thank you."

The pig said,
"Scratch my back,
oink oink
please."

"Oink oink thank you."

Tom said,
"Read me
a story."

"Say please,"
said
Auntie Bea.

"Woof woof,
quack quack,
meow meow,
oink oink,
please."

"Woof woof,
quack quack,
purr purr,
oink oink,
thank you."